Dedicated To Alex, And All Other

Faced With A Unique Set Of Circumstances.

Every Child Is Different.

Every Child Is Special.

No Child Is Alone!

Written by Luke Dalien

Illustrated by Linnae Dalien

Mark's mommy and daddy had struggled to explain
what was happening to Mark's muscles causing the pain.

Sure this seems simple to some
who are older and understand
why their legs hurt sometimes,
even when they don't stand.

But to Mark and his sister, who was only six-years-old,
it was tough to grasp what they were being told.

Mark's mommy explained that no two people were the same.

Starting with how each person has their own individual name.

Some people struggle to use their hands to write.

Other people can't use their hands at all,
though they try with all of their might.

Some people can't speak even a simple word like "my."

Other people can't stop talking and
even yell, though they don't try.

Some people's eyes don't work at all, even with light.

Other people's eyes have absolute perfect sight.

Some people need a chair with wheels
or braces on their legs to get around.

Other people can walk and run perfectly on the ground.

Some people can hardly lift a tiny object like a mouse.
Other people are so strong they can lift a small house.

Some people are quiet, though they can be loud.
Others don't know the meaning of
silence and enjoy a large crowd.

Some people enjoy writing and using their minds.

Others would rather use their hands to build. The world is
filled with all different kinds.

Some people get to choose what they can and cannot do.

"For you, Mark," his mommy said,

"your body made that decision for you."

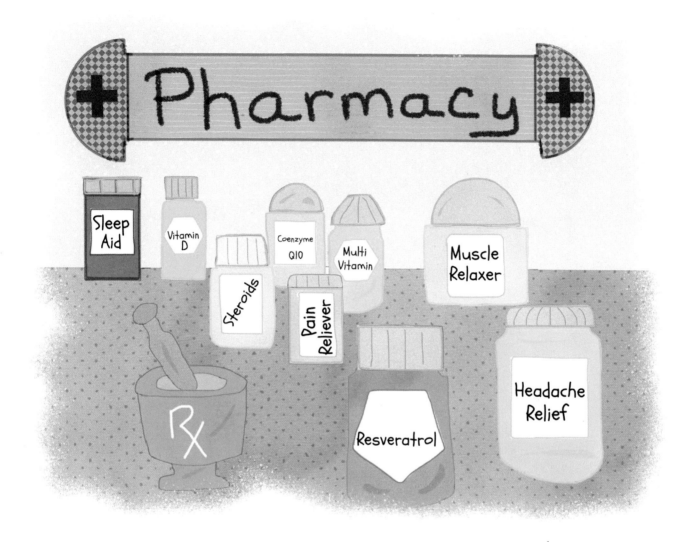

Sometimes there's medicine people
can take which will heal.
Other times medicine won't fix,
but can help the way they feel.

The truth is we are all completely
different both inside and out.
For that's what makes us unique,
and special... no doubt.

Mark and his sister nodded their heads,
as they began to understand
the differences we all have is the lesson at hand.

So the next time you see someone who looks
or acts differently than you remember, their body
was made in a unique way, and they're special too.

The End

Be sure and check out Luke's other books including:

Mark the Mighty Muskrat

The "Mark The Mighty Muskrat" series was created to help children understand extremely difficult situations. The books are created specifically for children (like the author's son) who have been diagnosed with a degenerative muscle disease called Muscular Dystrophy.

However, the lessons found within the series have proven to help children who have been diagnosed with ANY type of disease or disorder along with any siblings they have!

Do You Remember?

The "Do You Remember?" series is based on the unique path of life we are all fortunate enough to create. We often spend way too much time focused on things that do not matter in the end.

These books are designed to help children (and parents) remember the memorable aspects of life and the experiences that bring you together!

The First Series of Books by Luke Dalien

The Adventures Of The Silly Little Beaver

For fully animated versions of these books along with others written by Luke Dalien, please visit our website; www.LilexStudios.com

Author Luke Dalien has spent his life dedicated to helping others break the chains of normal so that they may live fulfilled lives. When he's not busy creating books aimed to bring a smile to the faces of children, he and his amazing wife, Suzie, work tirelessly on their joint passion; helping children with special needs reach their excellence. Together, they founded an online tutoring and resource company, **SpecialEdResource.com.**

Poetry, which had been a personal endeavor of Luke's for the better part of two decades, was mainly reserved for his beautiful wife, and their two amazing children, Lily and Alex. With several "subtle nudges" from his family, Luke finally decided to share his true passion in creativity with the world through his first children's book series, "The Adventures Of The Silly Little Beaver."

Illustrator Linnae Dalien grew up in Minnesota where she raised two adoring children with her husband, Larry. Always creative, she found her passion in designing and editing photographs until they achieve that "perfect look." It wasn't long before family and friends began reaching out requesting her to work on their own photographs for a variety of special occasions.

It was during that part of her life that her creativity took a turn and a new passion was born. Linnae discovered her true artistic ability as she began doodling and drawing different characters to aide in some of the photographs she was working on. Reaching out to her son, Luke, regarding her new found love for drawing, they decided to join forces and launched their first book series, "The Adventures Of The Silly Little Beaver."

For a fully animated version of this book along with others written by Luke Dalien, please visit our website; www.LilexStudios.com

LILEX STUDIOS

Made in the USA
Columbia, SC
29 June 2022

62503354R00018